U.S. HOLIDAYS

Celebrate Veterans Day

by Melissa Ferguson

PEBBLE
a capstone imprint

First Facts are published by Pebble,
1710 Roe Crest Drive, North Mankato, Minnesota 56003
www.mycapstone.com

Library of Congress Cataloging-in-Publication Data
Library of Congress Cataloging-in-Publication data is available on the Library of Congress website.
ISBN 978-1-9771-0265-2 (library binding)
ISBN 978-1-9771-0529-5 (paperback)
ISBN 978-1-9771-0282-9 (eBook PDF)

Editorial Credits
Mandy Robbins, editor; Cynthia Della-Rovere, designer; Pam Mitsakos, media researcher, Tori Abraham, production specialist

Photo Credits
Alamy: Pacific Press, 3 (bottom left), 18-19, Science History Images, 10-11; Getty Images: Bettmann, 8-9, Corbis, 12-13, Corbis/Robert Daemmrich Photography Inc, 20-21, Taxi/ Catherine Ledner, 6-7; Shutterstock: Anton_Ivanov, 14-15, Bokeh Blur Background, Design Element, BPTU, 4-5, Cheryl Casey, Cover, Duda Vasilii, Design Element, Olya Detry, 16 (bottom left), sharpner, 1 (bottom), Thorsten Schier, 17

Printed and bound in the United States of America.
PA49

Table of Contents

What Is Veterans Day?

On November 11, Americans celebrate the men and women who serve in the U.S. ***military***. This ***national*** holiday is called Veterans Day.

A veteran is someone who has been in the military. Many of them have served in wars. They fought to protect the country's freedoms.

military—the armed forces of a state or country

national—to do with or belonging to a country as a whole

Fact The Army, Air Force, Navy, Marine Corps, and the Coast Guard make up the U.S. military.

Veterans are often away from their homes and families. They face dangers in war. People who serve sometimes get hurt. When they come home, they may struggle with difficult thoughts and feelings.

American Freedoms

Americans have many *rights* and freedoms. They have freedom of speech. Americans are free to follow any religion or none at all. These freedoms were fought for and protected by veterans.

right—something that the law says you can have or do, as in the right to vote

Fact There are about 20 million veterans in the United States.

How Veterans Day Became a Holiday

Veterans Day started after World War I (1914-1918). World War I was called the "Great War." It was one of the biggest wars in history.

During World War I, about 8.5 million soldiers from around the world died. People hoped this would be the last war.

Fact More than 4.7 million men and women served in the U.S. forces during World War I.

U.S. army infantry soldiers fight during World War I.

World War I officially ended on June 28, 1919. But fighting stopped on November 11, 1918. The day became known as ***Armistice*** Day.

Americans celebrated with songs and parties. They were happy the fighting had stopped.

Fact On Armistice Day, the fighting ended at 11 a.m. on November 11. November is also the 11th month of the year.

armistice—a formal agreement to temporarily stop the fighting during a war

Americans in Philadelphia celebrate Armistice Day in 1918.

Armistice Day honored World War I veterans. But World War I was not the last war. Millions of men and women served in World War II (1939-1945) and the Korean War (1950-1953). Americans wanted to honor U.S. veterans from all wars. In 1954 Armistice Day became Veterans Day.

Fact There have been 26 U.S. presidents who served in the armed forces.

Before becoming president, John F. Kennedy served in the U.S. Navy during World War II. He is pictured here (center) with his crew mates.

Sites and Symbols of Veterans Day

Many Americans go to Arlington National Cemetery on Veterans Day. It is near Washington, D.C. More than 400,000 veterans are buried there. On Veterans Day, there is a ***wreath***-laying ***ceremony*** at Arlington National Cemetery.

wreath—a ring of flowers or branches; wreaths are often laid on graves or memorials

ceremony—special actions, words, or music performed to mark an important event

The Tomb of the Unknown Soldier

After World War I, the body of a soldier was buried in a ***tomb*** at Arlington National Cemetery. No one knew his name, but people wanted to honor his service. He is called the Unknown Soldier. Many other unknown soldiers have been buried there since then. Today soldiers guard the tomb at all times. This is how they honor the fallen veterans.

tomb—a room or building that holds a dead body

One important *symbol* of Veterans Day is the red poppy flower. During World War I, many soldiers died on Flanders Field in Europe. Months later, poppies began to grow there. The red poppy became a symbol honoring those who died.

Fact American Moina Michael started selling red poppies to honor veterans in 1918.

symbol—something that stands for something else

A field of red poppies in Germany

How You Can Celebrate Veterans Day

Many schools and offices close for Veterans Day. Some towns and cities hold parades. Many businesses offer free services to veterans and members of the military on that day. Americans proudly fly their flag.

Fact New York City holds America's biggest Veterans Day parade.

Veterans march in a Veterans Day parade in New York City.

You can honor veterans in many ways. Go to a Veterans Day parade. Send a letter to a veteran. If you see a military person, thank him or her. On Veterans Day, we remember those who have served the country.

Glossary

armistice (ARM-iss-tiss)—a formal agreement to temporarily stop the fighting during a war

cemetery (SEM-uh-ter-ee)—a place where dead people are buried

ceremony (SER-uh-moh-nee)—special actions, words, or music performed to mark an important event

military (MIL-uh-ter-ee)—the armed forces of a state or country

national (NASH-uh-nuhl)—to do with or belonging to a country as a whole

right (RITE)—something that the law says you can have or do, as in the right to vote

symbol (SIM-buhl)—something that stands for something else

tomb (TOOM)—a room or building that holds a dead body

wreath (REETH)—a ring of flowers or branches; wreaths are often laid on graves or memorials

Read More

Ferguson, Melissa. *Celebrate Memorial Day.* U.S. Holidays. North Mankato, Minn.: Capstone Press, 2019.

Koestler-Grack, Rachel A. *Veterans Day.* Celebrating Holidays. Minneapolis: Bellwether Media, Inc., 2018.

Ponto, Joanna. *Veterans Day.* The Story of Our Holidays. New York: Enslow Publishing, 2017.

Internet Sites

Use FactHound to find Internet sites related to this book.

Visit www.facthound.com

Just type in 9781977102652 and go.

Critical Thinking Questions

1. Why do we celebrate Veterans Day?
2. Do you think that the red poppy flower is a good symbol for Veterans Day? Why or why not?
3. What do people do to celebrate Veterans Day?

Index